THE FRENCH BRIDE OF ARKANSAS

MAIL ORDER BRIDES OF ARKANSAS

SUSANNAH CALLOWAY

D1737124

Tica House
Publishing

Sweet Romance that Delights and Enchants!

PERSONAL WORD FROM THE AUTHOR

Dearest Readers,

Thank you so much for choosing one of my books. I am proud to be a part of the team of writers at Tica House Publishing who work joyfully to bring you stories of hope, faith, courage, and love. Your kind words and loving readership are deeply appreciated.

I would like to personally invite you to sign up for updates and to become part of our **Exclusive Reader Club**—it's completely Free to join! We'd love to welcome you!

Much love,

Susannah Calloway

VISIT HERE to Join our Reader's Club and to Receive Tica House Updates

https://wesrom.subscribemenow.com/

CONTENTS

CHAPTER 1

The day had passed as so many days before it – with a long sigh of relief and aching muscles. Keith was silent as he overlooked the acres of property his father had secured for his family and regarded the expanse with pride. His work for the season was nearly complete, and soon the tobacco fields would be prepared for the winter. Harvesting was hard work, but once it was done, it would have all been worth it. The family would eat, and they would want for nothing for yet another year. And perhaps more than anything, his father would be proud of him.

He turned back toward the estate, which was a massive white colonial house that his father had built. In fact, his father had spent more than a year watching over the men that labored every day until the house was finished. Keith still noticed the small details of the house, no matter how much his mother had tried to change the décor over their years of living there. She could change the furniture, but she couldn't change the vision Keith's father had seen when the house was built.

His body felt stiff as he neared the front doors to the estate. Even so much as walking up the stairs was enough to cause his muscles to throb. He could hear voices coming from the front parlor as he ascended the stairs. He opened the tall red door and closed it behind him, only to sigh at the sight of the Charltons. That was exactly what he needed – company, especially after a long day out in the fields.

"Keith, there you are," his mother said, coming out from the dining room. "I was about to call to you in the fields. I invited the Charltons over for dinner."

There was a pang in his stomach. He was famished from having worked all day and was looking forward to eating a hearty meal. However, upon seeing the Charltons and their daughter, Beatrice, he couldn't think of a place he'd less like to be.

"Good to see you, boy," Mr. Charlton said, appearing shorter and stalkier than Keith remembered. "Been workin' hard, I see."

"Well, it's almost winter. Got to prepare the fields."

He watched as Beatrice tossed her curly hair back, peering at him as though he'd said something utterly ridiculous. "Why work out there when you've got workers of your own? Never made no sense to me."

There it was. The reason why he always tried to avoid Beatrice. She wasn't a particular looker, what with her round face that reminded Keith of her father, but she dressed well. With her parent's wealth came a personality he never warmed up to. She detested those who worked, and often looked down on those who were less fortunate than she. To top off everything, she was always gossiping about the other women in town.

"My father always said it was good to get your hands dirty from work," he told her, showing her his hands, which had been through the ringer and back and were covered in callouses. "Said it made you appreciate what you had."

"Well, I s'pose."

Mrs. Charlton took off her gloves and turned to Keith's mother, May. "Where is Simon, anyhow? I thought he was going to join us this evenin'."

"He should be here any moment. Keith, why don't you go wash up? I'll take the Charltons into the dining room. Join us once you're ready."

Keith clenched his teeth and gestured toward his father's library, which was just off the parlor. "Can I speak to you for a moment, Mother?"

His mother smiled to her company and gave her son a look

before stepping into the library with him. She leaned in close, as though the Charltons would be able to hear every word, even though they were in the other room.

"What is your problem, Keith?"

"Oh, don't you go an' play it that way. You know exactly what my problem is," he said, his voice sharp. "Why are they here?"

"Can't your mother have some company over without havin' to ask you? Besides, don't you like Beatrice?"

"You know exactly what I think of her. She's outright rude to those that she considers lesser than. Why would I want a wife like that?"

His mother pointed at him sternly, the wrinkles around her eyes deepening as she scowled. "You don't go sayin' a bad word about her now. She has all the makings of a good wife. She's decent lookin' enough, comes from a good family, and minds her manners. You could learn a thing or two from her, in fact. And you'll eat dinner with us tonight, you hear?"

"Ah, Keith, there you are."

Keith stepped around his mother when he saw his sister, Justine. She wore a long deep green gown with ruffles along the sleeves. Her blue eyes stared at the two of them inquisitively as she entered the library. "The Charltons are ready for dinner, and daddy's comin' in from the stables now."

7

"Thank you, Justine. Go on into the dining room," her mother said and turned to face Keith. "Go wash up, and then come join us."

Keith knew not to say another word against his mother. There were some fights that he just wouldn't win and choosing whom he was going to marry was likely to be one of them. His mother and father had a way of controlling where his money went, whom his heart went out to, and what his future would be.

He had a lot to be grateful for in life, but marrying Beatrice Charlton wasn't included, and he knew it. Voicing that opinion to those who considered her the best match for him in the whole area? Well, it was only going to fall on deaf ears.

Keith knew it had only been a little over a few hours that he'd spent in the company of the Charltons, but it felt like years. Their company was about as exciting as watching hay bales sit in stacks in the fields. His father sat at the head of the table with Mr. Charlton next to him, each appearing satisfied with the meal.

Keith leaned back against his chair and looked over the company, who were each too busy eating to notice that his family had, for the most part, finished their meals. The Charltons might have been decent when it came to their manners, but they were also intolerably boring when it came to conversation.

"I told a friend I'd go and meet him later tonight, so I have to get going," Keith said, and pushed out his chair. "My apologies. It was lovely to see y'all again."

"You didn't mention this before, Keith," Keith's father, Simon said, with a dark look shadowing his eyes. "Be sure to let us know next time. It ain't fittin' to leave the table when we have guests over."

Keith smiled to the company and ran his hand through his hair. "I'll keep that in mind next time, Pa. Have a good night, everyone."

He could hear his mother sighing as he left the room. The wood floors creaked beneath his weight, filling the silence he'd left. It didn't matter what was courteous at that point. Keith just knew he needed to get out of there. At that hour of the evening, there were only going to be drinks and monotone conversation, anyway.

He left the dining room and could hear the sound of footsteps approaching from behind him. He stopped and turned, only to see his sister rushing after him. He let out a deep breath, hoping she hadn't started agreeing with their parents. The last thing he needed was for his sister to take on the role of being upset with him when he made decisions for himself.

"What're you doing out here? You heard what they said about me leaving the table. You should head back," he told her.

"I told them I needed to wash my hands," she said, keeping her voice barely above a whisper. "There's something I need to tell you before you leave."

Keith took another step closer to his sister. "You seem pretty serious about this."

"I am, Keith. It's about your future with Beatrice."

Goodness, how he disliked that girl. "What about her?"

"I overheard Ma and Pa speaking earlier today," Justine said and glanced back to the door of the dining room, just in case. "They said they wouldn't let me marry Adam unless you married first. They're planning on arranging a marriage between you and Beatrice. I'm not sure when, but that's the reason they invited the family over tonight."

"You sure that's what you heard? Last thing I need is to get mad over gossip that ain't right."

"I know what I heard, Keith. They really do plan on it."

It wasn't long until his hands were shaking with building anger and resentment toward his parents. Their calculated ways of controlling his life were becoming ridiculous. And now they were using his sister's inability to get married to the man she adored. This was enough. He brought his hand into a fist and stared at the dining room door. He wanted to break it down and yell at all five of them.

"Thanks for letting me know, Justine. I'm headin' out," he said and brought his eyes to hers. "Can't say when I'll be back. Just let me know if you hear anything else."

She nodded softly and watched as he left the house, slamming the door behind him.

CHAPTER 2

The saloon was bustling with workers. He didn't need to wonder whether or not his best friend and oldest acquaintance, Jacob, was there. He was there most nights, enjoying the view of the servers who brought them their ales. Keith removed the hat from his head and slammed it down in front of Jacob, causing his friend to jump.

"What's goin' on with you?"

Keith took a seat at the bar next to Jacob and waited for the bartender to come up with a pint of ale. "What do you think? The Charltons are over right now, and I just found out my parents are making an undercutted deal for me to marry their daughter."

"No foolin'?"

Keith turned to his friend. "Ain't no joke, Jacob. My sister overheard everything and told me 'fore I left. Right done deal, apparently."

One of the men in the saloon took to the piano, filling the voids of conversation with a lively tune. Some of the girls were clapping to the sound, enjoying themselves, as the bartender placed a pint glass in front of Keith. He took a long swig of it, letting the bitter liquid wash over his tongue, savoring the taste.

"What're you going to do?"

Keith shrugged, not sure what to say. What could he do? "They're saying that they're goin' to make it so that Justine can't marry Adam unless I agree to marry Beatrice. They say I need to be married first."

Jacob brought his brown eyes to the pint in front of him. "That's a right shame. Yer sister's a sweet girl, and she sure cares about Adam. You know, I've been real happy with how things turned out between me and Chloe."

"And?"

"Well, I think maybe you should consider gettin' yourself a Mail Order Bride. I mean, heck, it worked well for me. We're even expecting our first child."

"What? Really? Congratulations, Jacob. Next round is on me."

Jacob gave him a large smile, causing his tan skin to wrinkle around his mouth. "Well, thanks. It was the best decision I ever made."

"So, you really think it'll work for me?"

"I think it might help in solving your problem. Your parents want you to marry Beatrice? Well, then, find a woman who's even better. At least, it would be your own decision."

Keith considered his words. It was a difficult proposition, but one that could possibly work. The thought of bringing a woman, one he'd never met, all the way to Rutger's Creek sounded like a mess waiting to happen. What if she hated the tobacco fields? It could also turn out that she was worse than Beatrice—though, that was unlikely. He brought the ale to his mouth and stared out across the bar at the number of whiskey and rye bottles along the shelves.

Then again, it could be amazing, and she could be everything Keith had ever wanted in a woman.

"You look like you're considerin' it. Good. I think you should do somethin' for yourself this time around," Jacob said, his voice low. "You do too much for your family already. The least they could do is accept the idea that you want to be happy with a woman. Trust me, Keith, there ain't anything worse than being trapped with a terrible woman for the rest of your life."

"But you just said Chloe was the best decision you ever

made."

"And don't you doubt it. I was talkin' about some of these other people you see luggin' themselves around in a sorry sort of way. You can tell their lives are a livin' torment by the women they chose to marry."

Jacob had a point. In fact, Keith knew men in Rutger's Creek who had taken the wrong woman to bed and forced to marry. They were a sorry lot who always came to the saloon after dark. He didn't want to be one of those men.

"Thanks for talking me through it, Jacob."

He watched as Jacob shrugged, nearly knocking his hat over. Yeah, Jacob had a way of calming Keith down when he was at his worst. All those years of being as close as brothers had forged a bond stronger than steel between the two.

The next morning was heralded in by the birds outside gathering to leave for the winter. Keith woke with a pounding head, and rolled over in his bed, trying his best to alleviate the pain that made him feel as though he'd been knocked over with a busted whiskey bottle. He grunted as he swung his legs over the creaky old frame and rose to his feet. The world spun for a moment as he gathered himself and pulled at the collar of his white shirt, which felt way too tight after sleeping in it overnight.

The air in the room was cold, bringing with it a shiver that swept over Keith's skin. He stretched his arms up in the air, feeling his shoulders and elbows crack as he limbered up for the day. A knock on the door caused him to turn around, peering toward the end of his room.

"Come on in."

He smiled when he saw Justine poke her face in, already dressed and ready for the day. She was always like that, even when they were younger. Early riser and first to bed. She took on much of the work of becoming the best version of herself, which Keith admired.

"You should really stop all this sleeping in," she said, taking a step into the room. Her pale-yellow dress added some much-needed color to the room. "How'd last night go? You're looking a little worse for the wear."

Keith shrugged, pulling up his baggy pants. "Well, I definitely learned from Jacob that things are going well with Chloe. So much so that he's expectin' his first child."

"You don't say," Justine said and clasped her hands together. "That's the best news I've heard all week. I'll have to stop by their farm and give them my regards."

"That you should. But you'll want to know what decision I've come to. It wasn't an easy one to make, but I think I should follow Jacob's lead."

She narrowed her eyes at him. "What're you talking about?"

"I'm talkin' about going to sign-up for a Mail Order Bride. The last thing I'd ever want to do is get in the way of your happiness," he said, and sighed. "I see the way you look at Adam. I know how much he cares for you, too. I want the two of you to be able to marry, and I refuse to take Beatrice as a wife. So, it's lookin' like ordering myself a bride is likely my best option."

Justine smiled softly, likely glad to hear Keith speak so highly of Adam. "You know what? Let's go into town together. I think it's best if I do the writing," she said.

"You sure you want to help me with this? Ma and Pa have no idea what I'm about to do, so you'd be an accomplice."

Her smile shifted into a sly expression. "Now, why would I want to miss out on all the fun? Besides, you'll need my help if you're looking to place an ad."

"All right, then. Get out of here and give me some space to dress. I'll eat quick, and we'll head into town. Just be sure not to say anything on your way out."

"And spoil you finding a wife? Never."

Keith watched as Justine left his room, feeling a sense of renewed hope. He wasn't sure what kind of woman would be arriving, or if there'd be one available at all. What he did know, however, was that it was his choice.

And there was merit in that fact alone.

CHAPTER 3

There was a sense of loss that came from a broken heart. It was as though a piece of her had been taken that day. She'd watched his shadow cross the floor as she sat against the wall, feeling crumpled from the defeat of having lost her beau. He'd left just as quickly as those words had been uttered – *I don't love you anymore.*

Colette brought her hand to her chest at the thought and stared at the now dwindling items she'd brought with her from France. He'd left her with little to no chance of surviving in America. By all means, she should've gathered as much cash as she could find and fled the country back to France. It would be difficult returning, considering there would be no parents there waiting for her—just the comfort of knowing she was back in the country where she'd grown up. Admitting defeat wasn't an easy thing for her to do. At this point, she had little less than a week to leave the room she'd rented, as there was no other way for her to afford it.

He'd already left with his portion of the money they'd brought together, and his own room across the hall was empty. She refused to even look at the neighbor who had moved into the room in his stead. There was no reason to – it only caused her more pain.

Colette lifted herself off the chaise lounge and peered out the window. It was growing colder outside since winter had started to break into the midst of autumn. There were leaves all along the ground, and there was the thrum of people passing the building outside.

Colette learned quickly that America had all types, and they often passed each other in the streets without so much as a word. Some women wore tattered garments that had scuffs of dirt along the bottom, while other women strolled by with hats that made them appear bigger than life. Colette sighed as the sun shifted from behind the clouds, illuminating the city. It was a shame to let such a beautiful day pass when winter was just around the corner.

She turned back toward her shawl and grabbed it off the back of a nearby embroidered accent chair. She wrapped the red shawl around her shoulders and inhaled deeply. Her hands were shaking at the thought of leaving the room without him. She'd barely taken any strolls throughout the city since he'd left. She'd remained cooped up inside her room, staring out the window with the curiosity of a child. She often daydreamed about the lives of those that passed, wondering if they were married, if they were happy, ailing or hardworking. She tried to read their happy or pained expressions as they passed.

She tried to think of a plan. Tried to figure out a way that she could make it in America alone. Her English skills were not very good, and she feared she would be rejected for any position she pursued.

She turned her face away as she left her room and saw the closed door across the hall—the room he had stayed in during their time together in America. That was before he had fallen out of love with her and in love with someone else. Colette gripped the fabric of her shawl and made her way down the near-claustrophobic hallway, descending the stairs.

This wasn't the best boarding house to stay in, but it was the best one they could find in the short amount of time they'd had after they first arrived. The owners were seldom seen, except for when they reminded Colette the due date for her next payment. The woman, a Mrs. Williams, had discovered the couple's falling out, and was right to assume that Colette couldn't afford the room on her own.

Colette was silent as she closed the front entrance door behind her and stepped out onto the busy street. New York City always had a grey overcast appearance to it and smelt of burning coal. It seemed like a downtrodden place unworthy of being the main port into America. Everyone arriving had the same auspicious expression on their faces when they first arrived, Colette included.

The sound of carriages passing caused her to walk down the sidewalk faster. She'd never looked both ways before crossing the street until she'd arrived in New York. It was there that she learned that having such a vast array of people also meant they each had different ways of transporting themselves throughout the city. Some rode on horseback, others in carriages, and some walked. The bustle of those that lived in the huge city always surprised her, as each person seemed to be frantically trying to get somewhere. She was unaccustomed to such haste, and always compared it to her own town just outside of Paris. There, it had been a leisurely place, where things were done in their own time.

She brought her shawl in closer as chills formed against her skin with the passing of wind. She began to feel the weight of no longer having somewhere warm to rest her head. Colette knew she had to figure out something quickly, or she'd soon suffer at the hands of an American winter, which she'd heard were always difficult. The wind blew, whistling alongside the sounds of hooves clattering against the ground and the conversations of passersby.

Her heart felt as though it would fall from her chest as she thought of what her future might entail. She stepped to the side quickly, avoiding a collision with a passing woman, and took a deep breath near the windows of a shop. The air was cool, despite the sun being warm against her skin. She watched, as she always did, as everyone passed her by. She received glances from men, no doubt because of her comely face, but she paid it no mind. She preferred to be invisible when she was distraught.

The wooden door next to her opened and she watched as a beautiful young lady stepped out with a massive smile grazing her lips. Colette furrowed her brow and turned to look inside the shop, which turned out to not be a shop at all. She'd heard rumors about such things in America, but she'd never seen one before.

This office was close to where she was staying, and she was surprised she hadn't noticed it before. There were a number of women in the parlor, standing at desks and filling out forms. She could see the sign above the desk, deliberately letting each woman know what they were signing up for – *Mail Order Brides wanted.*

Work had been difficult to find since she'd arrived in America. Her fiancé, Pierre, had managed to find work at a nearby factory. Colette, however, had been burdened with no luck since she'd arrived. A Mail Order Bride? She could easily read the words, and she knew what it meant.

Becoming a Mail Order Bride would provide her with the comfort and care of a home, without having to worry about work. She'd learned quickly that finances could destroy young love. She didn't want to experience it again.

If she *were* to become a Mail Order Bride, she'd also become a permanent citizen in America. Wouldn't she? She wasn't sure, but in any case, she wouldn't have to worry about no longer having family to rely on. She'd have married into one and would save herself the trouble of returning to France without so much as a penny to her name.

She pressed her shawl against her chest and meandered toward the door, nearly tripping over her dress on the way in. The voices of the women both in front and behind the desks were hushed, as though they were gossiping about someone in the room. Colette could only assume they were discussing personal information. Who knew why the other ladies were there? Were they desperate? Colette was surely in need, so she imagined that the other women were in a desperate situation themselves.

"Hello, miss. May I help you?"

Colette stopped as she neared the desk and turned to a homely lady with curled white hair pulled back in a braid. "Hello. I-I am sorry to bother you. I wonder what this Mail Order Bride thing is."

The lady leaned against the high desk and smiled. "Well, come over here. I won't bite. What kind of questions do you have?"

Colette peered around the room, unsure of where to start. "How does it work? Do you find a husband for me?"

"Exactly how you think it does," the woman said, and laughed. "We receive an advert, which is essentially someone asking for a girl to come down and marry them."

"And they fall in love?"

The woman's face fell somber at the sound of her words. "I'm afraid not all of them fall in love, dear. However, most of them do live comfortably. There are times when we women have no other options."

Colette could feel the tears forming in her eyes. She was one of those women. "I do not know what to do, but I am happy to apply for one that you might have. I think I could try it."

"Well," the woman said, and grabbed a packet of papers from beside her. "There are quite a few here but there's one that's asking for someone right away. Are you looking for a placement for the future, or right away?"

"Now or sooner, if possible."

"You're pretty enough that I don't think they'd send you back, neither. Take a look at this one," she told Colette, placing the page in front of her so that she could read it. "This one here is looking for a woman to head over to Rutger's Creek, Arkansas. Owns a tobacco farm, so he's sure to have money."

"Does it describe him?"

The woman raised her eyebrows. "They tend to leave out that part. I've heard the majority aren't much to look at, but aren't hideous, neither. You should be fine."

Colette stared at the piece of paper in front of her until the letters began to swell into a black mass of unreadable text. "Have you been to this place, Rutger's Creek?"

"No, miss. Can't say I have."

"What about Arkansas?"

The woman peered at Colette as though she'd said a joke. "I haven't done too much traveling. Not enough time for it."

"Were you a Mail Order Bride?"

She shook her head. "No, miss. But my daughter was, and that's part of the reason I started working for this agency. She's very happy with her life, and I felt it was necessary to help other women who've yet to find someone for themselves. It can also help you start a new life."

Colette considered the woman's words carefully. Start a new life? That was the reason she'd traveled with Pierre to America. They had so desperately hoped to begin anew and make their own family. Unlike Pierre, this man in Rutger's Creek already had money, so there was a good chance Colette wouldn't be strained to find a job. She would be able to start a new life on her own terms, free of the stress that had caused her engagement to fall apart at the seams.

"How soon do they be wanting someone there?"

The woman smiled widely and took back the page from the top of the desk. "As soon as two days, if you can manage it."

It was the largest decision Colette had ever made, but it also sounded as though it would be her best and maybe only option. She would walk into the situation head-on and survive as best as she knew how to.

"I will do it."

CHAPTER 4

Keith was returning his horse, Juniper, to the stable when he saw his sister Justine rushing up toward him through the barn doors. He could hear her panting and see her breath in the late autumn air. Keith closed the gate to the stable and turned toward her, watching as she tried to catch her breath.

"You all right, Justine?"

She held her hand out to him, as though to silence him as she caught her breath. He leaned against the top of the stall and felt the horse nudge his shoulder. He lifted his eyes to the massive black horse, its brown eyes seeming as though they were burrowing into his. He'd had Juniper for over five years by that time, and she'd been the best mare he could remember. There was something to be said about a hardworking, cooperative horse.

"Yes," she said, and smiled as she caught her breath. "I have some amazing news for you, Keith. Can you guess?"

He gave her a half-smile. "Well, I'm not sure if I can guess what it is. You seem rather taken with the news. I'd hate to ruin the surprise."

"Well, it's about the Mail Order Bride," she scoffed, narrowing her eyes at him. "We've gotten a reply to your advert, and the letter said that a beautiful young French woman will be arriving in about a week."

A beautiful *French* woman? He tried to think what that could entail. Keith was sure he'd only ever heard one man speak French, and he'd sounded like he'd drank too much moonshine in his life. Hopefully her voice wasn't quite as raspy as all that.

"Beautiful? How're you sure that she's beautiful?"

Justine shrugged. "I don't know, Keith. That's just what the letter said. I mean, I doubt they'd lie in their letter."

"I wonder if they told Jacob that Chloe was beautiful, too."

"It's possible."

Keith considered what this woman might look like. There were all kinds of faces passing through his mind, of women who'd traveled through Rutger's Creek that he'd considered to be beautiful. There hadn't been that many that'd traveled past, but he could see the women's faces as clear as day. If the

French woman looked anything like those women, he wouldn't be able to help but drop to one knee and profess his love right then and there.

"So, are you going to tell Ma and Pa?"

He blinked himself back into the barn and shook his head. "No, Justine, that's not a good idea. You know how they are. It's best if we just keep it a secret for now. Just between the two of us until things set themselves straight."

"You're forgetting something."

"What do you think I'm forgettin'?"

She gestured to the barn, and Keith stared at her until she huffed. "Where's she going to stay, Keith? She can't stay here if she's a secret."

She was right. Keith hadn't really considered that, as everything had happened faster than he'd expected. There was no way she could stay with the family without his parents being apprehensive, and if she stayed in town, there'd be gossip abounding about the new girl that he was visiting while in town. That didn't leave many options, except maybe the person who'd suggested the whole situation.

"I might be able to convince Jacob to let her stay with him and Chloe."

"Do you think he would agree? I mean, she might be

surprised when she shows up to find that she's staying with your friends instead of you."

Keith waved away her words. "Naw, it won't be a problem. I'm sure she'll be well taken care of there, and I'll be sure to cover her expenses until the wedding."

He saw a sly smile form on Justine's lips. "So, you're really going to do it?"

"What choice do I have now?" he asked her and chuckled to himself. "She's already on her way here. No goin' back."

Jacob lived close to his parent's plantation, and reaching his farm wasn't too difficult. Keith took the well-trodden road, feeling the cool breeze against his skin as he felt Juniper's movements beneath him. He could already see them outside in the distance, tending to their land alongside their workers. That was one of the things he admired about Jacob – he always worked the lands, just as Keith often did himself. Keith had always considered it the honorable thing to do, as it showed that you really cared about your land.

He watched as the men dissipated as a group and meandered on to separate sides of the land. He could tell who Jacob was from his signature hat, which was holding still against his head, despite the strong winds. Keith brought up his hand and waved at his friend from the top of his horse, waiting for

Jacob to notice him. In his peripheral vision was a young woman with light blond hair, who stepped out of the modest house with her hand on her stomach. Seeing her brought a smile to Keith's lips. His friend was living his best life, and he couldn't be prouder.

Jacob went to fetch Chloe, and Keith turned Juniper down the path that led to their house. He watched as they both waited for him along their dark oak porch. He could tell that his friend was in love with his wife. Even the way he looked at her as she held her hand against her growing stomach was enough to convince Keith that he himself was making the right decision.

Keith waved as he and Juniper trotted up to the porch. "Hey, you two."

"Keith," Chloe said, and waved to him lightly. "What brings you here?"

"I have somethin' I have to ask of you two."

Jacob heard those words and immediately reacted with a broad smile. He stepped forward to the railing and leaned his forearms against it. "What'd you say, Keith? You askin' for a favor?"

Keith had known Jacob would be that way. He loved having people owe him things and hated accruing debts of his own. In the time that he and Keith had been friends, he'd never had any issues with gambling or fighting.

"Yes, you heard me right. I'm askin' you for a favor, Jacob."

"Well, I'll be," Jacob said, and tipped his hat. "Mark this day, Chloe. It's finally happenin'. Keith Hamilton is goin' to owe me."

Chloe giggled. "That'll be a first since we met, that's for sure. What do you need, Keith?"

Keith was silent for a moment. Looking at their property, he was sure that they could use the help that an extra set of hands might be able to provide. As long as he paid for his bride's food and lodging, there shouldn't be a problem. Still, there was a strike of guilt in his stomach at the thought of forcing them to take in someone they didn't know. All because Keith was making decisions without his parent's approval. It caused him to feel selfish.

"I don't want to force this on you both, so if you find it to be any trouble, you should tell me."

"Well," Jacob said, leaning forward. "You have to tell us what you want before you assume that we can't do it. I know we'll do our best to help you out, if we can."

Keith inhaled deeply. "I didn't tell you, Jacob, but I went ahead and put in an advert for a Mail Order Bride. She's to be arrivin' here within a week or so, but I can't have her stayin' with me and my folks. See, they don't know she comin' right now, so she'll need somewhere to stay," he said, feeling his jaw tighten with his words. "I was hopin' she could stay with you until we get things settled with my family."

Chloe brought her hand to her mouth, clearly elated by the news. "My goodness, that's wonderful, Keith. Of course, we'll welcome her here. In fact, we could use as much help as we can get."

"See?" Jacob asked, and reached forward, nudging Keith's shoulder. "Whatever the lady says goes, so you have your answer. We might need help with some supplies, considering it'll be winter soon, but if you're willing to help pay her way, there shouldn't be any trouble. Besides, it ain't likely to be long."

"There's no issue there, Jacob. I already had that in mind," he said, and shifted Juniper so he could get a better look at Chloe. "Thank you, Chloe. Let me know if there's anything I can do while you're expecting."

"I'm sure she'll help out just fine, Keith. Let us know when she arrives to town. I'll get one of the spare bedrooms ready in the meantime."

Seeing Chloe be so welcoming was only more of a nudge in his chest that Keith had made the right decision. If this young lady arriving was anything like Chloe, he'd find himself to be a very lucky man.

CHAPTER 5

Colette was awakened by the train attendant, and she felt the cool window against her cheek as her eyes fluttered open. The sound of the train whistle reverberated throughout the train car, and she sat up in her seat, holding onto the window ledge as the train came to a stop. She could feel her stomach lurch forward as she caught herself. She worked to lift her luggage from beneath her seat. She avoided the eye contact of the other passengers as she gathered her things. Rutger's Creek was a small stop, and she soon realized she was the only person leaving the train.

She was silent as she passed the other benches, peering out the window toward the broad view beyond. The leaves beyond the small town had already started to fall from the trees, and it appeared as though they were a sea of multicolored gems, ranging in rich colors she'd rarely seen before. Bright canary yellows, deep scarlet reds and bright oranges swayed in the wind. Interspersed between the dense trees were small houses and farmland.

Her hands started to shake as she neared the exit. She wasn't sure if she'd really made the best choice. What if he was a horrible man? What if he was ancient, and rude, and repulsive? Her heart thrashed in her chest as she took the first step onto the platform and the male attendant helped lower her black luggage down onto the ground next to her. She could feel the chill in the air the moment she stepped out. It was colder than she was expecting as she moved along the platform, searching for anyone with a sign or a welcoming face.

There was no one.

The attendant closed the door behind her, and she watched as the train blew its whistle and the black smoke entered the air above it. Colette brushed her dark brown hair behind her ear and brought her jacket close to her chest to block out the cold air.

"Colette?"

She stiffened at the sound of the female voice. She'd fully expected a man, not a woman. Colette bit her lip and spun around, nearly knocking her luggage over. The girl before her was young, but not too much younger than Colette. Maybe just a few years. She had soft features, reminding her of a daisy.

"What luck! I was nervous I'd miss you."

Colette watched as the young woman put on a big smile.

"Hello. I am Colette."

The girl gave a small laugh as she reached the part of the platform where Colette was standing. "Well, of course you are. There ain't no one else here except you."

"I think you are right," Colette said, and scanned the area, realizing that she was the only person on the platform except for the young woman. "And who are you? I am sorry. The agency only gives me the information in the advert."

"Oh, I actually wrote that."

Colette's heart sank in her chest, and she thought she was going to be sick. Had this young woman done this out of spite for Mail Order Brides? Maybe her friends had put her up to it to get a laugh? She wasn't sure how to feel about the situation. She'd been made to look rather foolish. And beyond that, what now? What was she to do?

"Don't worry, though. I only helped my brother write that," she said, and placed her hand on Colette's shoulder. "My name's Justine. I'm Keith Hamilton's younger sister."

Colette let out a sigh of relief. "*Mon Dieu*. I am sorry, but I am thinking that I make a terrible mistake."

"I don't want to make you worry at all, Colette. Let me assure you that my brother is a fine young man. In fact, you're doing us a great favor just by being here. Now, then, why don't you come along with me? There's some people for you to meet."

"When will I meet your brother?"

"And please, just call me Justine. And you'll meet him tonight at dinner."

Colette furrowed her brow as she lowered herself to grab her luggage. She followed Justine silently, still unsure of the situation she'd gotten herself into.

The farm was smaller than she'd expected, but she was happy to have a place where she would belong. They pulled up in the carriage and Colette sniffled, her face reddened and numb from feeling the cold wind against her skin on the way there. Justine grabbed her luggage for her and placed it on the ground next to the carriage. Standing there, Colette saw a couple exit the house with smiles on their faces. She wasn't sure what to expect, but it was certainly not a young couple.

Justine led Colette up toward the porch that rounded the entire house, which was all made of dark oak timbers. It appeared to be an older house, but there was no doubt that it seemed homey and comfortable.

"You must be Colette," the young woman from the house

said, extending her hands to take Colette's hands into her own. "I'm Chloe, and this is my husband, Jacob."

She glanced from the man with the hat to Chloe and felt her cheeks flush. "*Mon Dieu.* I was not thinking so many to live together."

Justine laughed behind her. "We don't live together. This is Jacob's farm," she said, rushing down the stairs to grab Colette's luggage. "You'll be staying with them for the time being. Just until things settle."

"Ahh," Colette said, unable to find the right English word to say.

Chloe squeezed Colette's hands in hers. "I, too, was a Mail Order Bride. For Jacob. I know how you feel right now, and it's okay. We'll take care of you."

Colette smiled softly, glad to have someone who could understand. It would be nice to be able to have someone so close that could help her during her time transitioning into her new surroundings. There was a glimmer of kindness in Chloe's blue eyes that made her feel at ease, finally allowing her to relax slightly.

"*Merci*, Chloe. I thank you."

CHAPTER 6

The fields were nearly finished. Keith peered over the workers, making sure that they weren't becoming too exhausted. He stepped next to a young man he'd hired at the beginning of summer and joined him in pulling at the plants himself. It needed to get done before the first snowfall. It was the biggest harvest they'd had since his grandfather had started the plantation, and it was a great feeling to get into the work. It set his mind at ease from everything else that was going on in his life.

He placed the plants next to his feet and heard telltale footsteps nearing him. Justine had always had a skip to her step that he could detect from a mile away. He brushed the cold sweat from his forehead and turned to face her. It was obvious from her excited expression that she had good news.

That was enough to set Keith at ease. He trusted her opinion, and it only made him excited to hear her news.

"How'd it go?"

Justine held her hands at her chest, trying to hold back a smile. "She's beautiful, Keith. She seems nice, but a little shy. Not that I blame her, as it must be so hard to leave her family and come all the way out here."

"And you like her?"

"I do, but what does it matter what I think?" she asked and shook her head. "It only matters what *you* think. Be sure to dress up tonight when you meet her at dinner. You can't go looking like you do now."

Keith glanced down to his worn and dirty outfit. His brown pants were covered in bits of soil and his white work shirt was covered in smears of the tobacco he'd pulled from the ground. "You think there's something wrong with this outfit?"

She squinted her eyes at him. "Of course. You can't meet her wearing that. It matters that she likes you, too. So, make a good impression."

"Fine. I'll see about changin', then."

"Also," Justine said, just as she was about to spin away, "thank you for all of this, Keith. I know it's not the easiest decision to have made, but I really appreciate what you're doing."

It warmed his heart to hear those words from her. She didn't wait for his reply, and instead rushed toward the house. Justine had never been good with admitting things or telling people how she felt. But if she was grateful, that was enough for him. Besides, he hadn't done this solely for her...

Keith's heart was pattering in his chest as he stepped toward the entrance of Jacob's house. He could hear the voices from inside and felt his nerves firing. He wasn't sure whether he wanted to meet her at all. He was curious about how beautiful she was, but there was no telling if they would get along. What if she was like Beatrice?

Justine knocked on the door before he was able to walk away, and he heard footsteps nearing the door. He held his breath as Jacob opened the old, creaky door and welcomed them inside with a smile.

Jacob neared Keith and leaned in close, his hat brushing against Keith's hair. "You ready to meet your bride?"

Keith gave him a look, knowing that he didn't even need to reply. He just wanted to meet her and find out what he'd really gotten himself into.

Justine hugged Jacob as Keith wandered out of the entryway and toward the dining room, where he heard glasses clinking against the table. He saw Chloe, whose blond hair was braided up toward her neck. He didn't recognize the young woman beside her, whose back was to the doorway.

Keith cleared his throat, not knowing what else he could do to get their attention. His blood was rushing through his veins, causing him to feel lightheaded. He caught his breath when she turned around to see who was there.

Her expression reminded him of a doe. Large, hazel eyes set in a delicately soft face widened the moment she saw him. Her skin reminded him of ivory, and her brown hair was curled and pinned up around her face. She was more than he'd expected. In fact, she might have been one of the most beautiful women he'd ever seen.

"Y-you must be Colette," he said, his voice wavering. "My name's Keith. Thank you so much for traveling all this way."

Colette lowered her eyes, her face flushing red. "Thank you, Keith. *Oui,* I am Colette, and it is much pleasure to meet you."

She was delicate, and he couldn't help but feel as though she were the opposite of a woman like Beatrice. That enough was obvious. There was, however, the question of whether he was ready to make her his wife. Would his parents accept her? Could they forge a future together, as Jacob and Chloe had?

He took a step closer and turned back as he heard Justine laugh at something Jacob said behind him. If it meant that

Justine would be happy, he could do it. He could do anything.

Colette's mornings spent at the Miller's farm were quiet and relaxing—especially after the kitchen chores were finished. There was a sweetness to the house, especially with the excited buzz of a child on the way. She sat next to the window and practiced reading an English book, mouthing the words so that she could practice her enunciation. Hearing their accents compared to hers was difficult. She was so strongly aware that the way she spoke was different from them. There were even times when Jacob had a difficult time understanding what she was saying. The least she could do was practice her English in her spare time.

Colette peered out the window and watched as the first few snowflakes began to fall along the top of the mountains in the far distance, hovering above the trees like great pillars. She was silent as she watched the snow fall, feeling a gripping sensation in her chest. She missed France, and everything familiar that lay in her home country.

She could hear Jacob and Chloe speaking together at the table at the other end of the room, enjoying their warm tea. She kept her eyes toward the window, thoughts racing through her mind. In the time she'd been there, she'd had many opportunities to speak with Keith. They were always small, light conversations. It was as though the four of them all been friends for years, even though Colette had only been there for little more than a week.

Each time he visited; however, she had the sensation that he couldn't bring himself to feel anything for her. She wasn't sure if it was because he wasn't interested, or if he wasn't ready to take her as his bride. He was handsome enough and, from what Jacob had told her, he was the heir to a successful plantation. He wanted for nothing – except that he wanted to make sure his sister was happy. Her happiness was one of his few wants in life from what she could surmise. The one thing she could tell about Keith was that he cared deeply for his sister and his friends.

There was an audible gasp that nearly caused Colette to drop her book. She brought her eyes to Chloe, who was holding onto her stomach with a loving expression on her face. She watched as Chloe took Jacob's hand in hers and brought it to her midsection, where he began to smile so big, she thought his face might get stuck that way. There was an expression that passed between the two that caused Colette's heart to skip a beat.

"He moved," Chloe whispered softly, chuckling. "I think I can feel him kicking."

It was difficult for Colette to see them together so happily. She'd had that once – with Pierre. They'd admired each other in the exact same way. That was, of course, before his love was shifted to another woman. The heart could be foolish and make decisions based on a whim. She was happy for the couple, but she couldn't help her own frustration.

She made the choice, then, that she would accept Keith however she could have him. Love didn't entirely exist for her. She'd thought that such a thing was real when she'd experienced it. But looking back on it, she couldn't say any longer whether her love for Pierre was real. In the end, it was only two people making poor decisions and hurting each other, even if there had been some happy moments in between.

CHAPTER 7

It was the first time Keith would visit Colette in the afternoon. Of course, there was some attraction there on his end, but he wasn't sure how their relationship would unfold from here. In the time that he'd been visiting, things had often been awkward. When it was just the two of them, the conversations were stagnant, and they were unsure of how to proceed. It was disheartening. Having heard from Chloe and Jacob how well their whirlwind romance had been the moment she arrived, it made things seem distressing. What if they never came to care for one another?

Keith debated his future as he entered the house, having already spoken to Jacob outside. The air in the house was warm as he closed the door behind him. From what he'd heard, Colette kept mainly to herself, always peering out the window and practicing her English. He hadn't overlooked her accent, but it wasn't as bad as he'd been expecting. There was no throatiness in the way she spoke, as he'd expected. Her voice was soft and demure, much like she was.

He stepped into the doorway of the dining room and found her at the chair where Jacob said she'd be sitting. The sunlight cascaded in from the window beside to her, causing her skin to appear as luminescent as snow. Her hair had fallen lightly along her face as she stared out toward the vast expanse of forest just beyond the farm.

"Colette?"

She brought her hazel eyes to him and raised herself to her feet. "Keith? I not know you were coming today."

"Not goin' to lie. Came here to surprise you," he said, and walked toward her. "I heard you've been stayin' in while you've been here, so I thought it'd be nice if we went for a walk. What do you think?"

Colette brought the book from the chair next to her and placed it on the window ledge. She moved the fabric of her pink dress aside and placed her hand in the space between them. "That would be lovely. Did you have a place in your mind? Do I need to change my dress? This not right for me to wear?"

"No need for changing. Just come along with me."

She smiled as he took her hand and placed it on his arm. He led her through the house, gathered her cape, and went out into the wintry air, able to see their breath as they walked. He could see Jacob in the distance, preparing his own fields for winter. There were voices beyond them, workers speaking about what they would be doing next.

"So, are you enjoying Rutger's Creek?"

Colette was silent for a moment, peering out toward the mountains along the horizon. "It is most peaceful here. I did not really like New York City very much. It is too busy."

She wrapped her hands around herself and gave a light shiver as they walked. Keith stopped and took off his jacket. The least he could do was be a gentleman.

He placed it over her shoulders, only to have her hold still, as though he was about to hug her. She pulled the jacket in closer and he let out a breath, hoping he hadn't overstepped any boundaries.

"*Merci.* It is getting too cold. I have fear my cape is not enough."

A silence passed between them as they stood apart, yet close, to one another. It was the most time they'd spent alone together since she'd arrived in Rutger's Creek. Her hazel eyes met his before she turned away and blushed, causing Keith to return to the moment.

"Thank you for coming all the way here, you know," he said, watching as his breath fogged the air between them. "I know this must be difficult for you. It's really appreciated."

"*Oui,* your friends have been kind to me. I could not have asked for more better hosts while I am here."

Keith smiled at her words. "That's really nice to hear, Colette. You know, I intend on introducing you to my parents soon. When they're ready. As you might know, this whole Mail Order Bride business is a little difficult for some people to understand."

She gave him a quizzical look.

"Not that they don't approve," he lied, trying to take back his words so that she wouldn't worry. "It's just that it needs a little more time."

She started walking again, and softly stepped past him. He wasn't sure what else to tell her. The last thing he wanted was to scare her off and have someone awful to take her place from the agency. He fully intended on breaking the news to his parents the first appropriate moment he could find. He just needed to wait until that time presented itself, which was likely to happen when the Charltons weren't on his mother's mind.

CHAPTER 8

The town of Rutger's Creek was a quaint one. It was Colette's first time leaving the farm to browse the wares in town, and she was excited to see what kind of stores they had there. Just being out in public was enough to cause Colette's heart to beat a little faster. Despite her shyness, being stowed away in that house for so long had caused her to crave being around people.

She'd been practicing her English intensely for over two weeks and was already feeling more confident about speaking to strangers. With Chloe's help, she'd even managed to change the way she enunciated her r's.

She and Chloe walked through town with their arms interwoven, and Colette took in the sights of the town. The buildings were a mixture of old and new, with new properties appearing throughout town. She could hear the piano music emanating from the saloon as they passed, and Chloe waved to people that she knew. It seemed as though Rutger's Creek surely was a small place. Colette continued to spark people's interest. She could feel their eyes watching her as she walked alongside her new friend.

"Maybe we should go this way," Chloe said, pointing down an empty walkway. "There's a store on the other street. They sell fabrics."

Colette peered down the walk, which was nestled between a cobbler's shop and a house. "I am not sure that is necessary. We can continue walking the streets, *non?*"

Chloe appeared disheartened. Colette wasn't stupid – she could tell that Chloe was looking to escape something. What it was, Colette couldn't tell. She peered around the near-empty street and considered who she might want to avoid. It was then that her eyes landed on a young woman with a stern profile. She was heading right toward them.

"Are you not want—"

"Hello, Chloe. My goodness, how nice it is to see you out and about," the young woman said as she approached. Colette could tell the girl came from wealth. It was dripping from everything she wore and the way she held herself. Colette had only ever seen that kind of confidence in young ladies who knew their family's worth. The woman was staring at her. "Now, I'm sorry. We haven't been properly introduced. It's rare to see strangers around these parts."

Chloe stepped forward before Colette could answer, too hastily for it to appear casual. "Beatrice, this is Colette. She's a friend from out of town, and she's helping me with my pregnancy. You know how we need extra hands since mine are already full."

Beatrice turned to Colette and scoured every facet of her, from her feet to her face. Colette felt as though she was being critically judged, but for what reason, she didn't know. "Well, isn't that nice. How are you enjoying Rutger's Creek, Colette?"

"It is nice, thank you."

"Oh," Beatrice said, grimacing slightly, "you have an accent."

"*Oui*, I am French. I came to America about five months before."

"How nice."

Colette glanced to Chloe, who appeared fixated on Beatrice. It was a strange feeling that washed over Colette as she watched, as though Beatrice were searching for something. Obviously, she had an issue with people from out-of-country. That was fine enough. Colette had heard that the more rural communities were slightly closed off to foreigners. There was something else in Beatrice's expression, though, that caused her to feel uneasy.

"Well, ladies, it was quite lovely seeing you today. I must go," she told them, still peering at Colette with an expression Colette couldn't quite place – perhaps a mix between dissatisfaction and curiosity. "It was lovely making your acquaintance, Colette. I'm sure I shall see you again."

Colette smiled softly. "*Oui*, I hope I will."

Beatrice gave them a false smile as she passed, still gazing at Colette as she made her way down the road. Colette could see the wet mud along the hemline of Beatrice's dress as she watched her walk away. Even the most beautiful of garments still accumulated dirt, she thought, just like everything else.

She kept silent as Chloe took her arm in hers again and brought her toward the fabric store, where she would be choosing new fabrics to make baby's clothes. Chloe's silence worried Colette, but she did her best to keep her apprehension to herself. There was no reason to question Chloe – Colette trusted her deeply. It was the coldness in the air that Beatrice had left behind that worried her most.

She'd never heard Beatrice's name mentioned up until that point, and couldn't help but wonder what kind of person she was that she caused those around her to become anxious. Was it the thought that Beatrice would gossip about her?

Colette let out a deep breath and shook her head. There was no reason to worry. She had done nothing wrong, and Beatrice had no information for which to gossip with. It had just been a brief meeting. Nothing more, nothing less.

For the first time since she'd arrived at the Miller's farm, Colette had been asked to make dinner. It had been a few months since she'd cooked anything, but she was sure she could deliver a meal that everyone would like. She could already hear the voices of the guests in the dining room and could feel her heart quivering in her chest. There was quite a bit riding on it, even if it was just a dinner. She had to cook the perfect meal that would convince Keith that she was capable of performing her duties as a wife.

Not only that, but she intended to excel at them all. She was to be given a home when she had none to go to, after all. It was the least she could do.

She stirred the pot filled with cream of potato soup, all fresh from the market that morning with milk from the cows on the property. She turned back toward the main course, which would be lamb roasted with rosemary and thyme and potatoes. It was a simple dinner, but it filled the kitchen with a rich aroma. The closer it got to her serving the meal, the more excited she became to see everyone's reactions. She had always been a good cook. It had been too long since she'd cooked for someone else. Not since Pierre.

She breathed out softly and gathered the bowls and plates. She began preparing the meal for display, but there was no real way to make it look good in the old porcelain bowls and plates. It was clear that Chloe and Jacob had spent so much time tending to other matters, they hadn't gone out to purchase new silverware or porcelain. Well, Colette would make do.

She rounded up the bowls for the first course and gently kicked open the door to the dining room, smiling at the company gathered around the table. She saw that Justine was sitting next to a young man, whose personal care was impeccable, much like the young lady's. His blond hair was perfectly combed back, and he wore an immaculately tailored leather vest and white shirt. It was apparent that he, too, had money. It was strange for Colette to be around people who owned their own land – her family had always just made do. Everything they owned, however, had caused them to be indebted to others. She wondered if that was just the European way as she set down the first bowl in front of the young man.

Justine smiled broadly at her as she placed her soup in front of her. "Colette, this is Adam. He's my fiancée."

Colette greeted him with a smile and a nod. She was careful not to spill the last of the soup as she placed the last bowl in front of Keith. She was more than aware of everyone's gaze on her. She peered around the room, searching for Chloe. She needed a more friendly face. Being in the same room as Keith and his family was nerve-wracking.

"It is much pleasure to meet you, Adam," she said, trying her best to restrain her own French accent. "I hear many great things about you from Justine."

"Well, I've heard some great thing 'bout you, too, Colette," he said, and brought his hand to Justine's, wrapping his fingers around her palm. "We can't thank you enough for coming out here to Rutger's Creek. I can only imagine how different it must be to New York City, or even France."

"There are some things the same, but *oui,* it is most different."

Keith pushed his chair out and raised himself to his feet. "Let me help you with the rest of the dishes."

Colette nodded silently, overly conscious of his tall stature behind her as they entered the kitchen. She dished up the rest of the meals to their plates and watched as Keith left for the dining room with several plates in his hands. There was a sweetness about him that she couldn't deny, and he was far from bad looking.

Still, they hadn't been capable of building a bond since she'd arrived. Each moment felt a little forced, and it was distressing. She hadn't known what to expect when she'd arrived, but she had been hoping for a spark to be felt between the two of them. She could live without love, but she couldn't live without considering her husband her friend, and they'd barely been able to manage that much.

She grabbed her own plate and exited out into the dining room, only to see that Chloe and Jacob had made themselves comfortable at the table. She placed the last two plates in front of them, smelling the roasted lamb emanating in the air as she took her seat at the side of the table.

Chloe held her stomach as she overlooked the meal with a gentle smile on her lips. "This looks lovely, Colette. You outdid yourself."

Colette waved off her compliment, feeling her cheeks flushing red. "It is nothing, really. *S'il vous plait*, everyone, enjoy."

She jumped at the sound of Keith's gentle moan. Colette watched as he chewed the food in his mouth. She couldn't tell by his expression if he was pleased, or if he was forcing himself to eat the food she'd prepared. He'd gone straight for the roasted lamb and potatoes, without even so much as trying the soup, as one would expect him to do in polite society.

"This is right tasty, Colette," he said, still chewing his food. "One of the best meals I've ever had."

The rest of the table mirrored his sentiment, and she couldn't help but feel proud of herself. It was the first time cooking for her future husband, and he had been pleased with it. That was enough for her.

CHAPTER 9

Keith was pacing along Jacob's front porch, his breath easing into the air in front of him like smoke from a pipe. He could feel Jacob's eyes on him as he paced, unsure of what to say. The meal Colette had prepared had been created with such meticulous care that he couldn't help but feel indebted to her. There had been a tenderness to what she had made, and he could sense it the moment he'd taken his first bite.

"Your pacin' is not gonna do you any good, Keith."

Keith let out a deep breath. "I need to do somethin' for her. Somethin' real nice, you know? I'm just thinkin' about what I can do. You have any ideas?"

Jacob shrugged. "You could make her a nice dinner, like she did here tonight."

"You know I can't cook."

"Why don't you take her out somewhere? You could make a night of it."

Keith tapped his foot, considering the places in town, unless Jacob meant a place that was a considerable distance away. There was no way he could take her out to the saloon. That was certainly not the kind of place you took a woman like Colette.

"Why don't you go to my parents place in town? I can talk to them and set somethin' up for just the two of you."

"You sure that wouldn't be askin' too much of them? I don't mind payin' them, that isn't the problem. I feel as though we'd be interrupting their evening."

Jacob adjusted his hat. "You know, it seems like you're catchin' somethin' for this girl, and I don't mind helping you get to know her a little better. My parents would be fine with it, too, I'm sure. You worry too much."

"I'll need to make you a list. I'm hopin' to make it a really nice night."

"That we can do. You know, she's been real helpful round here ever since she arrived. I'd be happy to help you out and make sure Colette has a nice time," Jacob said, and chuckled to himself. "Now quit pacin' on my porch. You're making me uncomfortable."

Keith stopped next to Jacob and patted him on the back. "Thanks, Jacob. I sure appreciate it, you know. Everything."

He waited outside on the balcony, which was perfectly set up for their evening. He could smell the sweetness of the flowers he'd placed on the table as he stood in the empty space. Jacob's parents owned an inn in the middle of town and had rooms available for those who passed through Rutger's Creek. It was the perfect place to have a quiet evening with just the two of them.

He heard her footsteps outside the door and inhaled deeply, trying to ease his nerves. He held his breath as she opened the door. He was taken aback by how put together she looked. Her brown hair was braided back, and her face was exquisite, with just the right amount of pinkness in her lips and cheeks. It appeared as though she had taken every effort to look as beautiful as she could. It worked, and it took his breath away. She really was one of the most beautiful women he'd ever seen.

"Thanks for comin'," Keith said and rounded the table, pulling out her chair for her.

Colette peered around the room, her cheeks flushing. "Whose inn is this?"

He couldn't blame her for being apprehensive. Them being

alone in a room could be considered taboo, but it was the only way he could think of having an evening alone to get to know her. He'd made sure that everything was set up properly not to give her the wrong idea.

"This inn here belongs to Jacob's parents. I've ordered dinner for us, and it should be coming up soon."

Colette took a seat in the chair and kept her eyes on him as he sat at the table across from her. The room was filled with the scent of flowers, and candles had been lit in every corner. She sat down and waited for the food.

There was always a slight pressure between the two of them that didn't diminish – it followed each time they were together, as though it were a ghost lingering in the room. Keith cleared his throat, hoping to relieve the room of its tension.

"I wasn't too sure what kind of food you liked, so I started off with some bread, and then we'll be eating stew afterwards. Do you like wine?"

"I love wine. We drink wine in France."

Keith smiled, having at least gotten something right. "Well, expect some good wine tonight, then."

The door opened and Jacob's father, Steven, entered the room. He was a large man with an even larger beard. "Hello, Keith. And you must be Colette," he said, and placed two glasses on the table. "I've brought you some bread and wine to start. Let me know if you're craving something else, and I can see what I can bring up."

Colette nodded. *"Merci."*

Keith wasn't sure if she was impressed by the gesture of the evening, but he hoped she was. A lot of effort had been put into it by Jacob's family, and it hadn't been cheap. Not that he cared about the cost – it was worth it if it made her happy.

"Also," Keith started, pouring her a glass of wine, "these flowers are yours to take home this evening."

She leaned forward, smelling the roses that had a mix of wildflowers in the bouquet. "They most lovely. *Merci*, Keith."

He grinned with pleasure.

"So why you do all this?" Colette asked.

Keith poured them each a glass of wine and placed the bottle on the table. "I thought it might be a nice idea for us to get to know one another. Whenever we spend time at Jacob's, we're always surrounded by so many other people."

"I agree," she said, and held up her glass for cheers. "To a very good evening."

They clinked their glasses together. It was a small gesture, but it was enough to set the mood for the rest of the evening. Colette, without having known, had solidified in Keith's mind that she was the kind of modest woman he could see himself settling down with.

CHAPTER 10

The wind whistled between them as they made their way back to the Miller's farm. Night had appeared in Rutger's Creek, and everything had fallen quiet, save for the sounds of the forest beyond the farmlands. Keith held Colette's warm hand in his own as they walked, making sure to walk fast enough to force away the cool air and warm themselves up.

"Thank you for all you did," she said softly as they made their way down the path that led to Jacob's home. "I like it very much."

Keith held Colette's flowers in his other hand, and she could hear the petals rustling against his jacket as they hurried along. "I'm glad you enjoyed yourself. That's more than enough for me. I was a little worried you wouldn't like any of the food."

"Food is not a lot different in France."

"No? I thought it might be real gourmet."

Colette laughed softly. "*Non*, not at all. In some places, *oui*. But not at all the places. It is like here in America."

By the time she looked up again, she realized they were nearly at the porch. Time seemed to pass by quickly whenever she was with Keith. It was a bittersweet moment, for she didn't want the evening to end. Their conversation, though strained at times, had allowed her to get to know him just a little better. The idea that he'd spent time planning their meal and creating such a lovely atmosphere was touching.

"Well, here we are," he said, as they reached the bottom of the stairs to Jacob's house. "I guess that's it."

"*Oui*."

Colette startled at the feeling of Keith's hand against her chin. Her heart raced as he stepped closer to her. He was warm, and she wanted to embrace him against the cold more than anything. He lowered his face toward hers and she felt his lips softly touch hers. It was brief, but it caused her stomach to flutter.

She breathed in, as he pulled away, not having realized that she'd held her breath at all. It was as though his soft kiss had marked her lips and she could still feel the warmth of them against her skin.

"Have a nice night, Colette. Sleep well," he said, handing her the flowers.

She was flustered. Unable to speak, she merely nodded and held the flowers to her face, trying to hide the redness of her cheeks in the lamplight streaming from the window. She curtsied and wandered up toward the stairs, feeling as though she were floating. It lasted all the way until she fell into her bed, unable to bring herself back down to the ground.

The pang of guilt struck his chest like lightning. He knew that he'd let it go on for too long, having kept Colette hidden at the Miller's farm for a little over a month. Yes, it was clear that everyone was getting along, but it was only a matter of time until Colette started growing apprehensive about the situation. She was there, after all, to get married. Not to help his friend's wife with her pregnancy.

He knew that keeping her in the dark, as he had been, would eventually cause the situation to come apart at the seams. He couldn't allow things to end terribly. The air was cool in the barn as he gathered the hay, tossing it into the stables for the horses. He tapped his foot against the ground and decided that the time was narrowing down. He had to make the choice, and it was coming up soon.

He'd introduce Colette to his family. The concept of having brought in a Mail Order Bride had been for his sister. His dear sister, for whom he'd always cared so deeply. Her happiness meant that he could rest easy. Having met Colette, and gotten to know her, he couldn't deny that there was a skip to his heart at the thought of her.

He was ready to settle down – if he could do so with her.

It was only after his daily chores that Keith decided he would finally reveal Colette to his parents. The time had come to open up his world to Colette and invite her in. The decision wasn't easy – he knew that his parents would have a difficult time accepting the idea that he'd gone behind their backs. Whatever it was that they decided to do, Keith knew that he'd made the right decision for himself.

There was a silence in the parlor as he walked inside. His parents were on either side of the room, his mother at her writing desk, and his father reading over a few articles. The pages turning were the only sounds in the room, aside from his footsteps as he neared them. Keith cleared his throat, feeling the words trapped already.

His father kept his eyes on the pages in his hands. "What is it, son?"

Keith could feel the weight of the tension in the room, as though his parents knew that he was about to tell them something important. There was a chance that it was all in his head, but there was something about their studied nonchalance that caused him to feel uneasy. "There's something I'd like to tell you both."

"Well, out with it," his mother said, spinning around in her chair. "If this explains your behavior over the past couple of weeks, I'm eager to hear it."

Keith smiled nervously at his mother. "It does, Ma. It's real important; because I have a dear friend I'd like you to meet in the next couple of days. I'd like to have her over for dinner, if that's all right with you both."

His father relinquished his book, placing it down on the ornately decorated sofa. "A dear friend, hmm? And who might this lady be?"

"Her name is Colette."

He watched as his father turned to his mother. There was a look shared that seemed to confirm Keith's suspicions. Someone must have said something to them both. It wasn't as though his going to the Miller's farm was a secret, but the reason why was certainly kept under wraps. Or so he'd thought.

"Well, if she's *dear* to you," his mother said, emphasizing her words. "I see no reason as to why we can't open our doors to her for dinner."

"And you, Pa?"

His father shrugged. "I suppose it don't hurt none. By all means, let her know that we'll have her over, say on Thursday."

"Thank you. I know you'll like her, she's nice."

He left before the silence overwhelmed him. There was a heaviness in the air between the three of them. It was culpable, but Keith was now determined. He wouldn't let their disdain for the situation deter him. He'd make things work out. Somehow.

CHAPTER 11

Snow had arrived in Rutger's Creek. The air was filled with a deep chill that swept through Colette's dress as she made her way down the path. It had stopped snowing in the meantime, and she saw no reason why she couldn't walk to the property. That, it seemed, hadn't been the best idea. She hadn't taken in just how cold the wind would be. But it was too late now. She'd insisted on making her way alone to Keith's home since it wasn't all that far. She had determined that the time alone would help her muster up her courage.

Colette sniffled as she neared the property, unable to conceal her awe at the size of the colonial house in front of her. She'd heard that Keith was wealthy, but this was unlike anything she had expected. The property resembled the snow in its white starkness, heralding to her like a mountain at the end of the path.

Long hills rolled on either side of the property, likely where the tobacco was planted. All was covered in a thick layer of snow. She'd lost the feeling in her feet as she neared the massive house. The sound of the snow crunching beneath her feet caused goosebumps to form along her skin.

She looked up to see Justine's face in the front window, smiling at her. It was enough to reassure her that the evening would go well. As long as Justine was her usual self, everything would be fine. Still, Colette could feel her stomach knotting at the thought of meeting Keith's parents. She'd been working on reducing her accent and working on her English. There was still the nervousness that came with speaking, and she was sure that Keith's parents would ask her many questions throughout dinner. It was enough to cause her heart to race.

Colette made her way up the stairs as Justine swung the door open. Colette could already see that the inside of the house was just as incredible as the outside. She saw ornate furniture and paintings of what were surely ancestors along the walls. Colette brought her hands to her face and breathed into them, trying to regain all sensation in her limbs from the cold.

"I can't believe you walked here. There was no need, you know," Justine said, and closed the door behind Colette. "I'm so glad you made it, though. We've had a wonderful supper prepared just for the occasion."

Colette blushed, and peered around the entryway to the house. There were stairs ahead of her, ascending to a second floor. Along the stairs was a rich red velvet carpet and a number of paintings along the walls. It was the largest house she'd ever walked into. Each part of it solidified the wealth of the family in her eyes, and she grew all the more nervous. She wasn't, after all, from a wealthy family. She expected that they would ask her about her family, and she'd soon be at a loss for words.

She heard footsteps nearing her, and saw an older couple approaching. The wife had on a beautiful blue gown, and her husband had a finely tailored black suit with a gold pocket watch chain hanging from one of his pockets. She felt their eyes on her, scrutinizing every inch of her. Colette wished, in that moment, she hadn't walked.

"Well, now," the older woman said, scouring Colette as though she was inspecting a meal. "You must be Colette. Welcome to our home."

The tone in her voice was telling, and Colette wasn't sure why the lady seemed displeased. Still, Colette forced a smile. "*Merci* for invite me."

"My name is Simon Hamilton, and this is my wife, May. We're pleased to have you over, Colette."

Colette gave a brief curtsy. "It is much pleasure to meet you both. You have a beautiful home."

May Hamilton narrowed her eyes at Colette, causing her to feel uneasy. "I'm sure *you* would think so."

There was a tone to her voice that caused Colette to glance about the room, searching for an answer from everyone's expression. They all appeared as though they hadn't even noticed the older woman's odd attitude, which stunned Colette. Had she always been so rude to those she welcomed into her home?

Colette inched closer to Keith, who had appeared at her side, wanting to get some kind of support from him. She needed a gesture, a look, something that would convince her that her being there wasn't an issue. Unfortunately, she received nothing. His expression maintained a stoic appearance, his strong jaw clenched at the situation.

There was a knock at the door that caused Colette to jump. Everyone turned to May Hamilton, who straightened herself and smiled briefly at the sound.

"Who could that be?" Justine asked, furrowing her brow. "I thought it was just going to be us dining this evening."

"Well, I thought it would be nice to have some extra company," May said, brushing past Keith and Colette. "So I invited the Charltons."

Colette could see that Keith had stiffened at the sound of the name. There was a game being played, and Colette felt as though she was a pawn amidst it all.

May opened the door to the company and took in the young woman who walked in through the door. Colette instantly recognized her as the young woman she'd met while in town with Chloe. It wasn't that her face was entirely memorable – it was the air with which she walked that was unmistakable. She was similar to Keith's mother in her attitude.

May Hamilton took the young lady's hands in hers, smiling to the rest of the group in the entryway. "How nice of you to join us, Beatrice. I see you brought your mother," she said, and peered over Beatrice to an older woman with a distinct broad nose. "So nice to see you, Jane. Was Arthur unable to make it?"

The welcome was wholly different than what had been given to Colette; it was apparent to everyone in the room. Colette could tell that Keith was apprehensive if not downright annoyed with the situation, as well. His expression, though remaining the same, had a glint of anger in it. Colette brought her hands in front her, wishing she hadn't come to the Hamilton estate at all.

"Arthur is preoccupied this evening, I'm afraid. But it was no trouble for Beatrice and me to come on down here," Jane said, and peered over May, stopping slightly to grimace at Colette. "Thank you so much for having us."

May chuckled and led them toward the dining room without stopping to introduce them to Colette. "You know you're always welcome here."

Both Simon and May led their two visitors to the dining room, leaving Keith, Justine, and Colette to their silence. Colette felt as though she would burst out in tears from the interaction she'd just witnessed. She should not have been there. Not in the least.

"Don't worry," Justine whispered to her, placing her hand on her shoulder. "My mother and father will come around. This is only temporary."

"It's ridiculous," said Keith.

Colette turned to him, whose hand was clenched into a fist.

"It is fine," Colette said, and took in a deep breath. "They are just excited about their visitors. Come, we shall make this a most nice evening."

She could feel Keith's eyes on her as she walked toward the dining room with her head held high. She wanted to crumple onto the ground like an autumn leaf, but she couldn't allow them the satisfaction. Colette had been in similar situations before in France with women of a higher social ranking. Women detested those they considered below them. It was a natural occurrence, and Colette knew that giving in and admitting defeat was letting the women get the best of her. She'd do her utmost to keep up appearances.

"So," Jane said, taking a seat at the table next to her daughter. "I see you have another visitor."

May chuckled lightly. "Oh yes, please forgive me. This is a

friend of my son's. Colette, this is Beatrice and her mother, Jane."

Beatrice smirked at Colette as she took a seat at the table, with Keith taking the seat next to her. "I've already met Colette, actually. Didn't we meet in town? Chloe said that you were helping her with her duties at the farm, since she's with child."

Colette did her best to force a smile, despite feeling the tension in the room which seemed to be directed completely at her. Having Keith sit next to her relieved her nerves somewhat, but she wished she could disappear. "*Oui*, I remember. How very nice to see you again."

Keith's father stood up at the end of the table, just as Justine was pulling out her chair. He held a glass of whiskey in his hand and was peering at everyone in the room. "Well, I have some news this evening. I've just been made aware from Jane that we've a match that's been made," he said, his lips forming into a wide smile. "Now, I have to tell you, I was worried about my son finding himself a good match, but I couldn't be prouder to announce this here to y'all tonight."

Colette felt her heart thrumming in her chest. The expression on Beatrice's face was telling, and she wasn't sure how to decipher it. Colette wasn't expecting Keith's parents to cause a fuss over meeting her for the first time. No, something had gone awfully wrong.

"Arthur has agreed to allow his lovely daughter Beatrice to be wed to our son, Keith."

Colette felt her heart leap into her throat. She looked to Beatrice, whose smirk had grown at Arthur's words. Colette had endured enough. That was the last thing she could withstand – the whole thing had been a farce, and she'd been made to look like a fool. She pushed out her chair and curtsied to the group, holding back the tears that formed in her eyes.

Silently, she left the room. She could hear their voices, primarily Keith's, speaking all at the same time. The words, however, were muffled. She didn't want to hear anymore. She needed to leave.

Colette ran toward the doorway once she was out view of the company and stood outside for a moment, gathering her nerves. The cold wind was the only thing to greet her the moment she left the house. Darkness had crept up on the estate and night had arrived. She brought her hands across her chest, feeling as though her heart were being squeezed. She could hear footsteps nearing her and didn't bother to look.

"I'm so sorry Colette," she heard a voice say behind her, as the door to the house closed again. "I really had no idea that was goin' to happen."

She turned to Keith, feeling the cold sting of her tears

streaming down her face. "You had no idea? I cannot believe you. I think you know this was to happen."

"I knew my parents wanted to set me up with Beatrice, but I had no idea they were going to do it tonight. You have to believe me."

She could see the sincerity in Keith's eyes, but it was difficult to accept when she was so upset. "You make a fool out of me."

"It isn't like that at all," he said, his tone lowering. "I really didn't want for any of that to happen. I knew that bringing you here might cause some issues, but I thought they'd be more understanding."

"What do you mean? I do not understand this issues? You have not told me anything since I arrive here."

"And that's my fault, not yours," he said, bracing himself against the wind. "The truth is, you were meant to replace Beatrice. I don't want to marry her. You've seen what she's like. There's no way I could ever be happy with a woman like that."

"So this is why you want a Mail Order Bride? To go against what your parents want?"

"Yes, and I'm sorry for not telling you sooner."

Colette shook her head and sighed. "You can take me back to

the Millers. I do not want to be here any longer. This has been too much for one evening."

Keith lifted his hand to her, but Colette instinctively pulled back. This was what Pierre had done, and now Keith. Just as she was beginning to allow herself to fall for someone again, her heart was stomped on yet again. It really had been enough. Just looking at him caused her heart to break a little more.

It had always been a farce—she just didn't know it. *Love* was a farce, and she would never allow herself to be the fool again.

CHAPTER 12

Colette didn't wait for the next morning to pack her things. There was no point in having to face the Millers. Colette sat at the writing desk and began to write her note, trying her best to remember her English spelling. She had to make a concise, well-written letter to thank them for all of their generosity. The Millers had taken her in and treated her like family.

It was with a heavy heart that she signed off after explaining why she was leaving the way she was. She wiped another tear from her eye and placed the note at the end of the bed. Her belongings were already prepared in her suitcase, and she was ready. There was no more reason for her to stay.

She lifted the heavy baggage with both hands and silently crept through the house, making sure not to wake anyone on her way out. The silence followed her as she closed the door to the Millers' house a final time.

The wind swept her hair in all directions as she stepped off the porch. The snow hurdled against her like the waves of an ocean, but she resolutely battled on, doing her best to get to the end of the Millers' path. All she had to do was get to the station. From there, she would be warm, and she would be on her way back to New York City. America had nothing left for her.

She would go back to her home country of France, starting out where she had left off – with a broken heart and shattered hopes.

Keith was sitting in the dining room, unwilling to move. After he'd returned from dropping off Colette—insisting that he take her home even though she fought against it, it had felt as though the world had crashed around him. He didn't want to face anyone else. Even so much as looking at his parents was enough to cause his anger to rise. The way Colette had been treated still seared through him, causing his stomach to churn.

He lifted his eyes when he heard Justine enter the room. Her expression was solemn, and her eyes were downcast. He leaned back in his chair, unsure of what to say to her. There didn't seem to be any words that could right the situation he'd caused.

"I'm sorry about what happened tonight. I wish I'd known."

"It's not your fault, Justine," he told her, trying to keep his voice from wavering. "It's my fault. I messed up this whole situation by lyin' to everyone."

"I wouldn't say so. It's because of me that all of this happened."

Hearing his sister blame herself for it all caused his heart to shatter a little more. She was the last person to blame for everything. He jumped from his chair at the sound of the front door opening. He held his breath, hoping to see Colette enter the dining room once more.

It was Jacob.

"What're you doin' here?"

"I came as quickly as I could," Jacob said, trying to catch his breath. "It's Colette. She left this note and it seems she's left the farm, too. Don't know where she went, but she took all of her belongings with her."

"Did you see her leave?"

Jacob shook his head, which caused Keith to stand at attention. He had to go find her.

"There's a snowstorm comin' in, and it's not looking good, Keith. I'm not sure if she'll make it through the night."

Keith felt his entire body tense at Jacob's words. His friend was right. The chances of Colette finding shelter in a snowstorm were slim. "Justine, you stay here. I'm goin' to get my horse," he said, and brought his eyes to Jacob's. "Will you help me find her? I know it's askin' a lot, but I'll need the help."

"Of course, I will. I'm just as responsible for her as you are. Let's go."

Her breathing was shallow, and her lips were blue. Keith pushed in the blankets around Colette's body and kept the fire going, hoping that she'd wake from her unconscious state. The doctor was applying a cloth to her forehead, his lips pursed. The tension in the room was palpable.

"Well, we just have to wait now. You found her just in time," the doctor said, and shook his head. "Just be sure to keep her warm. That's all we can do for now."

Keith blamed himself. For all of it.

He brushed her hair back from her face and let out a deep breath. "Thanks for your help, Doc. I'll stay here with her and let you know when she wakes."

"I know you will," the doctor said, and gathered his bag. "Let me know if she gets a fever, too. I'll come back right away."

Keith lifted his eyes to the doctor and nodded. He was exhausted. The night had been disastrous, and he'd found Colette along the edge of the road, nearly covered in snow. If it hadn't been for her luggage peeking out from the top of the snowbank, he would've completely overlooked her. It was a miracle she was alive at all.

CHAPTER 13

It took two days for Colette to finally come to. Keith had been at the Miller's farm long enough that he'd made up a bed on their sofa on the main floor. He held his breath the moment she opened her eyes, and he took her hand in his.

Colette was flustered. She sniffled as she raised her eyes to Keith's and coughed lightly, still drowsy. Keith reached for the glass of water at her bedside and placed it to her lips. She lifted herself up slightly and took a sip. It seemed as though even the smallest of gestures exhausted what energy she had.

"How are you feelin'?" Keith asked her softly, pulling up the chair to her bedside to sit down. "You've been out for two days now."

Colette swallowed and laid back into the pillows. Her

breathing was sparse as she brought her eyes to the ceiling. "Two days have passed? I feel not good."

"You almost got hypothermia," he said, trying to keep his voice low. "You feelin' feverish at all?"

Colette shook her head.

"Well, that's good, then. It's somethin'."

"I did not make it to the station," she said softly, mostly to herself than to Keith. "I was foolish to leave. That snowstorm was so strong."

"It sure was."

A silence passed between the two of them. The sentiment from that awful night seemed to have impacted Colette to the breaking point, leaving her unable to get over what had happened. Keith had already talked to his parents, but she didn't know that.

"I'm real sorry about what happened, Colette. I owe you such an apology that I almost don't even know what to say," he told her, taking her hand in his. "Words can't make up for the way you were treated."

"It is not a good memory."

"Well, there's something I want to tell you. Will you hear me out?"

She brought her green eyes to his and nodded slowly.

"Now I'm not really good with things like this, but I need to tell you that I've come to love you, Colette. I don't want to marry anyone else. I want to marry you, and only you. I've let my parents know, and now they wish to apologize for the way they treated you."

Colette was silent, taking in each word as he said it.

"I need you to believe me when I say that I'm in love with you. I'm sorry for what happened, but I'm not sorry for requesting a Mail Order Bride. You're the best thing that's come around in such a long time. You've given me hope that I can have a bright future filled with love and happiness," he said, and bit his lip. "I'll understand if you want to go back to New York, but I'd be grateful if you chose to stay here with me."

He watched as Colette's eyes filled with tears. She squeezed his hand in hers. "Are you … are you meaning that, Keith?"

"Every word."

A soft smile formed on her wavering lips. "Then I tell you something, too." She coughed slightly and found her voice to continue. "I am loving you, too."

A wide smile broke out on his lips, and he felt the weight of the world lift from his shoulders. "Truly?"

"*Oui*," she said, in between tears. "Truly."

"So you'll stay?"

"I stay here ... with you."

He touched his lips to her forehead and his tears blurred his vision. "You've made me the happiest man in the Arkansas by saying that," he told her, unable to hold back his adoration. "I love you."

She smiled and closed her eyes. Exhaustion filled her.

But then, so did joy.

The End

CONTINUE READING...

Thank you for reading *The French Bride of Arkansas!* **Are you wondering what to read next?** Why not read *A Mother for her Birthday?* **Here's a peek for you:**

Gabe Douglas sat behind the scarred wooden desk in his office. He was the sheriff of Rutger Creek, Arkansas, and as such, he was taking advantage of a quiet day to go through some new wanted posters he'd received in the mail. He was tired, so he sat with his long legs stretched out full-length. Thank the Good Lord, today had been peaceful. His normally calm town had been stuffed with saloon fights, squabbles between neighbors, property disputes, and other disturbances lately. He was worn out from putting out all the fires the past few weeks.

Just for a moment, he let his lids fall over his silver-gray eyes.

The day was almost over, and he would be headed home soon. In the past, his wife, Mariah, would be there waiting for him, along with his daughter, Eva, and his mother. But no more.

Mariah had been gone for four years now. He was the deputy back then, and Mariah used to bring him lunch most days. She'd been in town with a basketful of fried chicken for him and the old sheriff, Mort McCombs, when all everything broke loose. A gang of bandits had tried to rob the bank and Mariah had been caught right in the middle of it. The first bullet fired killed her.

Gabe had managed to shoot and kill the man who'd shot Mariah, but revenge was a bitter trade for his wife's life. He'd never been the same, nor would he ever be again. Now his life was Eva and his job.

The door burst open and a skinny, older man rushed in. "There's a fight at Millie's Place. Come quick."

Gabe leapt to his feet and dashed past the man toward the roughest saloon in town. It was just a couple doors down, and he pushed through the saloon doors and strode inside. Men were gathered around egging the fight on, watching as two cowboys crashed into tables and slugged it out.

Gabe sighed in disgust and waded into the melee. "Break it up, you two. Break it up!"

Just as he put his arms out to physically separate the two, he caught a movement out of the corner of his eye and drew his pistol from his holster and fired. A man who'd drawn his gun gasped; his gun clattered to the floor and he clutched his arm where blood was beginning to stain his shirt.

Gabe turned and trained his gun around the room. "Anyone else got any funny ideas?"

Then he turned and grabbed each combatant by the shirtfront. "You two are going to owe Millie some damages, but right now you're going to jail. March."

VISIT HERE To Read More:

http://ticahousepublishing.com/mail-order-brides.html

THANKS FOR READING!

Friends, Don't Miss Any News

If you **love Mail Order Bride Romance, Click Here**

https://wesrom.subscribemenow.com/

to find out about all **New Susannah Calloway Romance Releases! We will let you know as soon as they become available!**

If you enjoyed *The French Bride of Arkansas,* would you kindly take a couple minutes to leave a positive review on Amazon? It only takes a moment, and positive reviews truly make a difference. Thank you so much! I appreciate it!

Turn the page to discover more Mail Order Bride Romances just for you!

MORE MAIL ORDER BRIDE ROMANCES
FOR YOU!

We love clean, sweet, adventurous Mail Order Bride Romances and have a lovely library of Susannah Calloway titles just for you!

Box Sets — A Wonderful Bargain for You!

https://ticahousepublishing.com/bargains-mob-box-sets.html

Or enjoy Susannah's single titles. You're sure to find many favorites! (Remember all of them can be downloaded FREE with Kindle Unlimited!)

Sweet Mail Order Bride Romances!

https://ticahousepublishing.com/mail-order-brides.html

ABOUT THE AUTHOR

Susannah has always been intrigued with the Western movement - prairie days, mail-order brides, the gold rush, frontier life! As a writer, she's excited to combine her love of story with her love of all that is Western. Presently, Susannah lives in Wyoming with her hubby and their three amazing children.

www.ticahousepublishing.com
contact@ticahousepublishing.com

Made in the USA
Monee, IL
12 November 2022

17562065R00056